The reproductions in this book have been made using the most modern electronic scanning methods from entirely new transparencies of Cicely Mary Barker's original watercolours. They enable Cicely Mary Barker's skill as an artist to be appreciated as never before.

FREDERICK WARNE

Published by the Penguin Group
27 Wrights Lane, London W8 5TZ, England
Penguin Putnam Inc, 375 Hudson Street, New York, N.Y. 10014, USA
Penguin Books Australia Ltd, Ringwood, Victoria, Australia
Penguin Books Canada Ltd, 10 Alcorn Avenue, Toronto, Ontario, Canada M4V 3B2
Penguin Books (NZ) Ltd, 182-190 Wairau Road, Auckland 10, New Zealand

Penguin Books Ltd, Registered Offices: Harmondsworth, Middlesex, England

First published 1944
Edition with new reproductions first published 1990
This edition first published 1999

1 3 5 7 9 10 8 6 4 2

ISBN 0 7232 4567 3

Printed in Dubai by Oriental Press

FLOWER FAIRIES
OF THE
GARDEN

❖

CICELY MARY BARKER

TED SMART

WHERE

Where are the fairies?
  Where can we find them?
We've seen the fairy-rings
  They leave behind them!

When they have danced all night,
  Where do they go?
Lark, in the sky above,
  Say, do you know?

Is it a secret
  No one is telling?
Why, in your garden
  Surely they're dwelling!

No need for journeying,
  Seeking afar:
Where there are flowers,
  There fairies are!

THE SONG OF
THE SCILLA FAIRY

"Scilla, Scilla, tell me true,
Why are you so very blue?"

Oh, I really cannot say
Why I'm made this lovely way!

I might know, if I were wise.
Yet—I've heard of seas and skies,

Where the blue is deeper far
Than our skies of Springtime are.

P'r'aps I'm here to let you see
What that Summer blue will be.

When you see it, think of me!

The Song of the Polyanthus and Grape Hyacinth Fairies

"How do you do, Grape Hyacinth?
   How do you do?"
"Pleased to see *you*, Polyanthus,
   Pleased to see *you*,
With your stalk so straight
   and your colours so gay."
"Thank you, neighbour!
   I've heard good news today."

"What is the news, Polyanthus?
   What have you heard?"
"News of the joy of Spring,
   In the song of a bird!
"Yes, Polyanthus, yes,
   I heard it too;
That's why I'm here,
   with my bells in spires of blue."

The Song of
the Periwinkle Fairy

In shady shrubby places,
Right early in the year,
I lift my flowers' faces—
O come and find them here!
My stems are thin and straying,
With leaves of glossy sheen,
The bare brown earth arraying,
For they are ever-green.
No great renown have I. Yet who
Does not love Periwinkle's blue?

(Some Periwinkles are more purple than
these; and every now and then you may
find white ones.)

The Song of
the Narcissus Fairy

Brown bulbs were buried deep;
Now, from the kind old earth,
Out of the winter's sleep,
   Comes a new birth!

Flowers on stems that sway;
Flowers of snowy white;
Flowers as sweet as day,
   After the night.

So does Narcissus bring
Tidings most glad and plain:
"Winter's gone; here is Spring—
   Easter again!"

THE SONG OF
THE FORGET-ME-NOT FAIRY

Where do fairy babies lie
Till they're old enough to fly?
Here's a likely place, I think,
'Mid these flowers, blue and pink,
(Pink for girls and blue for boys:
Pretty things for babies' toys!)
Let us peep now, gently. Why,
Fairy baby, here you lie!

Kicking there, with no one by,
Baby dear, how good you lie!
All alone, but O, you're not—
You could *never* be—forgot!
O how glad I am I've found you,
With Forget-me-nots around you,
Blue, the colour of the sky!
Fairy baby, Hushaby!

The Song of the Tulip Fairy

Our stalks are very straight and tall,
　　Our colours clear and bright;
Too many-hued to name them all—
　　Red, yellow, pink, or white.

And some are splashed, and some, maybe,
　　As dark as any plum.
From tulip-fields across the sea
　　To England did we come.

We were a peaceful country's pride,
　　And Holland is its name.
Now in your gardens we abide—
　　And aren't you glad we came?

(But long, long ago, tulips were brought from
Persian gardens, before there were any in Holland.)

The Song of
the Cornflower Fairy

'Mid scarlet of poppies and gold of the corn,
In wide-spreading fields were the Cornflowers born;
But now I look round me, and what do I see?
That lilies and roses are neighbours to me!
There's a beautiful lawn, there are borders and beds,
Where all kinds of flowers raise delicate heads;
For this is a garden, and here, a Boy Blue,
I live and am merry the whole summer through.
My blue is the blue that I always have worn,
And still I remember the poppies and corn.

The Song of the Pink Fairies

Early in the mornings,
    when children still are sleeping,
Or late, late at night-time,
    beneath the summer moon,
What are they doing,
    the busy fairy people?
Could you creep to spy them,
    in silent magic shoon,

You might learn a secret,
    among the garden borders,
Something never guessed at,
    that no one knows or thinks:
Snip, snip, snip, go busy fairy scissors,
Pinking out the edges
    of the petals of the Pinks!

Pink Pinks, white Pinks,
    double Pinks, and single,—
Look at them and see
    if it's not the truth I tell!
Why call them Pinks
    if they weren't pinked out by *someone*?
And what but fairy scissors
    could pink them out so well?

THE SONG OF
THE GERANIUM FAIRY

Red, red, vermilion red,
With buds and blooms in a glorious head!
There isn't a flower, the wide world through,
That glows with a brighter scarlet hue.
Her name—Geranium—ev'ryone knows;
She's just as happy wherever she grows,
In an earthen pot or a garden bed—
Red, red, vermilion red!

The Song of the Canterbury Bell Fairy

Bells that ring from ancient towers—
    Canterbury Bells—
Give their name to summer flowers—
    Canterbury Bells!
Do the flower-fairies, playing,
Know what those great bells are saying?
    Fairy, in your purple hat,
    Little fairy, tell us that!

"Naught I know of bells in towers—
    Canterbury Bells!
Mine are pink or purple flowers—
    Canterbury Bells!
When I set them all a-swaying,
Something, too, my bells are saying;
Can't you hear them—*ding-dong-ding*—
    Calling fairy-folk to sing?"

The Song of
the Shirley Poppy Fairy

We were all of us scarlet, and counted as
    weeds,
  When we grew in the fields with the corn;
Now, fall from your pepper-pots, wee little
    seeds,
  And lovelier things shall be born!

You shall sleep in the soil, and awaken next
    year;
  Your buds shall burst open; behold!
Soft-tinted and silken, shall petals appear,
  And then into Poppies unfold—

Like daintiest ladies, who dance and are gay,
  All frilly and pretty to see!
So I shake out the ripe little seeds, and I say:
  "Go, sleep, and awaken like me!"

(A clergyman, who was also a clever gardener, made
these many-coloured poppies out of the wild ones, and
named them after the village where he was the Vicar.)

THE SONG OF
THE CANDYTUFT FAIRY

Why am I "Candytuft"?
That I don't know!
Maybe the fairies
First called me so;
Maybe the children,
Just for a joke;
(I'm in the gardens
Of most little folk).

Look at my clusters!
See how they grow:
Some pink or purple,
Some white as snow;
Petals uneven,
Big ones and small;
Not very tufty—
No candy at all!

The Song of
the Phlox Fairy

August in the garden!
Now the cheerful Phlox
Makes one think of country-girls
Fresh in summer frocks.

There you see magenta,
Here is lovely white,
Mauve, and pink, and cherry-red—
Such a pleasant sight!

Smiling little fairy
Climbing up the stem,
Tell us which is prettiest?
She says, "All of them!"

The Song of the Snapdragon Fairy

Into the Dragon's mouth he goes;
    Never afraid is he!
There's honey within for him, he knows,
    Clever old Bumble Bee!
The mouth snaps tight; he is lost to sight—
    How will he ever get out?
He's doing it backwards—nimbly too,
    Though he is somewhat stout!

Off to another mouth he goes;
    Never a rest has he;
He must fill his honey-bag full, he knows—
    Busy old Bumble Bee!
And Snapdragon's name is only a game—
    It isn't as fierce as it sounds;
The Snapdragon Elf is pleased as Punch
    When Bumble comes on his rounds!

The Song of
the Lavender Fairy

"Lavender's blue, diddle diddle"—
    So goes the song;
All round her bush, diddle diddle,
    Butterflies throng;
(They love her well, diddle diddle,
    So do the bees;)
While she herself, diddle diddle,
    Sways in the breeze!

"Lavender's blue, diddle diddle,
    Lavender's green";
She'll scent the clothes, diddle diddle,
    Put away clean—
Clean from the wash, diddle diddle,
    Hanky and sheet;
Lavender's spikes, diddle diddle,
    Make them all sweet!

(The word "blue" was often used in old days
where we should say "purple" or "mauve".)

The Song of
the Gaillardia Fairy

There once was a child in a garden,
    Who loved all my colours of flame,
The crimson and scarlet and yellow—
    But what was my name?

For *Gaillardia's* hard to remember!
    She looked at my yellow and red,
And thought of the gold and the glory
    When the sun goes to bed;

And she troubled no more to remember,
    But gave me a splendid new name;
She spoke of my flowers as *Sunsets*—
    Then *you* do the same!

The Song of
the Sweet Pea Fairies

Here Sweet Peas are climbing;
   (Here's the Sweet Pea rhyme!)
Here are little tendrils,
   Helping them to climb.

Here are sweetest colours;
   Fragrance very sweet;
Here are silky pods of peas,
   Not for us to eat!

Here's a fairy sister,
   Trying on with care
Such a grand new bonnet
   For the baby there.

Does it suit you, Baby?
   Yes, I really think
Nothing's more becoming
   Than this pretty pink!

THE SONG OF
THE HELIOTROPE FAIRY

Heliotrope's my name; and why
People call me "Cherry Pie",
That I really do not know;
But perhaps they call me so,
'Cause I give them such a treat,
Just like something nice to eat.
For my scent—O come and smell it!
How can words describe or tell it?
And my buds and flowers, see,
Soft and rich and velvety—
Deepest purple first, that fades
To the palest lilac shades.
Well-beloved, I know, am I—
Heliotrope, or Cherry Pie!

The Song of
the Marigold Fairy

Great Sun above me in the sky,
So golden, glorious, and high,
My petals, see, are golden too;
They shine, but cannot shine like you.

I scatter many seeds around;
And where they fall upon the ground,
More Marigolds will spring, more flowers
To open wide in sunny hours.

It is because I love you so,
I turn to watch you as you go;
Without your light, no joy could be.
Look down, great Sun, and shine on me!